Living out of a Tin Cup

Printed in the United States of America.

December 2009

ISBN 978-0-9843838-2-5 (Soft Cover)

Magai New Media, LLC

P.O. Box 740

Rumson, NJ 07760-0740

www.magai.com

Dedicated to American soldiers killed in the line of duty.

You will never be forgotten.

Author's Foreword

People ask me *did you really write the book? Did you really take that photograph on the cover? Did you really create all the characters?*

I can only offer a qualified *yes*. Not because I am a plagiarist, but I only know that God had a story, and for some reason He chose me to tell it. So *yes*, I pecked away at the keys on my Apple, trying to interpret what the characters were telling me they really should be doing and saying, and I pushed the button on my iPhone to take the photo where God placed me during my travels.

My thanks to Ms. Pamela Raney and Ms. Roberta Rohde for their encouragement, support, ear and crucial editing, and also to another good friend (you know who you are!) who was honest enough to tell me exactly what he thought about the story. One needs such good friends.

The circumstances that gave rise to this story, which took a month from thought to publication, are best left for another day, maybe another book. When life gives you lemons, they say, make lemonade. My take on that is that when life gives you lemons, take 'em back and try to at least get store credit so that you can pick out what you really want.

Living out of a Tin Cup

My name is Rachel Sarnoff and I'm an FBI agent. I work on suspicious deaths, only some of which I solve, others I fail to do so, not because I am not good at what I do, but try as I might, I simply may not see that big flashing red arrow pointing to the villain.

If you have seen that quaint movie *Silence of the Lambs*, and like the particular prowess and haunting beauty of Agent Clarice Starling, played so nicely by Jody Foster, you will be disappointed upon meeting me. For starters, people who meet me in my professional capacity are most often already dead, and I do not go around parties loudly announcing *Hi, my name is Rachel Sarnoff, and I am an FBI agent.*

For that matter, I generally avoid parties. A few men, and a much smaller smattering of women, have commented on my looks, and sought my companionship but I have not taken them seriously, preferring to stay on the sidelines.

My mother chided me for stating that I prefer not to date people who would want to date me. No, I don't think less of myself, and I admit being picky, but it's my body, and I don't like sharing, so there!

I am the elder of two daughters born in the Ozarks of Missouri to a dirt-poor Methodist minister and his high-school sweetheart bride. We prefer to say *I'm from Missoura*, otherwise it sounds a tad too close to *I'm from misery*.

I like bragging that I am a honeymoon baby, but I only wish that it were so, since the county records don't lie, and no baby has ever been known to have gestated to just a bit shy of 7 pounds in a mere fortnight.

My papa hunted deer in the woods to feed us, and mama always thanked the Lord for his sure aim. He allowed me to load his gun and in return, I carried his backpack, and retrieved the spent casings so that he could refill them. I always remember the loud bang and the sharp smell of gunpowder. Once, and that was the very first and last time, I saw the buck go down in a spray of pink, and after that I made sure that my eyes were tightly shut until I heard papa's grunt of satisfaction.

It was a chance to be alone with papa, and made up for all of the Christmases where the stockings hanging on the mantle were emptier than my parents wanted. I would gladly trade every single Christmas or birthday present for just another day in the deep woods with papa.

My younger sister helped him dress the deer in our basement. She eventually became an obstetric surgeon, and is now working in rural China for the same ministry, delivering babies and spreading the Lord's Word when their government isn't looking too hard – they never really stop, you know. As I said, I am an FBI agent.

But this is truly not a story about me.

The Cinnamon Bear Cub of Bucks County

It takes a very daring, dedicated and morbidly curious person to even contemplate pumping a bear cub's stomach, even with the cutest of classifications – Cinnamon Bear - and doing so to find a partially digested human finger is guaranteed to make even the strongest to at least retch. But I'm getting a bit ahead of myself, so let me set the stage.

My friends at the Pennsylvania Game Commission tell me that there are over 15,000 bears. Every year during Thanksgiving, contrary to popular belief, turkeys are not the most hunted game in rural Pennsylvania – heck, just like the rest of you, most of us go to the grocery store for that and cash in our points – but roughly 1,500 bears get thinned by regulated hunting, making it the most hunted game in these parts. It helps if there is a light snow cover to make black bears about as easy to pick out as fish in a barrel, especially for the young, uninitiated hunters tagging along with their dads.

Although it is easy to roll the phrase *The Black Bears of Pennsylvania* off your tongue, not all of the Ursus Americanus are black; about one in a hundred is born cinnamon brown, giving them their name. Take heed that cutesy name does not make them any less dangerous, although they generally prefer acorns, berries, some vegetation, insects, small critters, fish and even carrion to humans. They den over winter, and that's when the cubs are born to the sows, as the females are called. By the next fall, the cubs are weaned and weigh over 60 pounds, but most often spend another winter with their mothers before parting ways during the subsequent spring.

Now Bucks County of Pennsylvania is not a popular habitat for bears, Black, Cinnamon, or otherwise, and starting on Columbus Day, which fell on October 13 in 2008, multiple sightings of a solitary Cinnamon cub pretty much dominated the news pouring out of Point Pleasant, PA, home of the Tohickon Valley State Park. To the new denizens of the area, mostly sophisticated expatriates from New York City, the big story was the darling little cub itself, with its beautiful fur, not any bigger than a dog; wilder and wilder yarns of its sightings and antics started popping up, but to the seasoned native locals, the big, unanswered question was - *where is the mama bear?*

By the end of the week, it became apparent that the cub was on its own. On Friday October 17, the park rangers of Tohickon Valley tranquilized the cub, and tagged it with a radio transmitter to study its travel habits. While the cub was down for the count, a magnet Biotechnology high school out of Freehold New Jersey won the nod to study its diet, especially since it had probably been recently weaned; some student got the notion to pump its stomach, and this is where the story really begins.

Of course, if they had only found berries and acorns, there would have been nothing more to see, but as luck would have it, there arose the matter of that group of high school coeds finding that partially digested human finger, to shrieks of *Eeek, No Way,* and *Far Out!*

A very thorough search of the cub's nails, fur, teeth and feces did not yield any evidence of an attack on a human, and nothing more of any relevance was found. It was now most imperative to locate mama, so that its own culpability in the matter could be examined. They released the tagged cub, and tracked its every move for a week, but it did not rendezvous with any other bears. Instead, it just meandered along the Tohickon Creek, which is part of a cold-water fishery well stocked with succulent trout.

In the meanwhile, extensive efforts were in progress to identify the owner of that finger, all of which yielded no results; hospitals and doctors did not report anyone unaccountably losing a digit, especially in the days leading up to October 17. No one was reported to be missing.

Thorough sweeps of the heavily wooded 600 acre Tohickon Valley region, conducted over two days with cadaver dogs in difficult terrain, did not turn up any bodies or body parts thereof. During the search, sundry articles of clothing, even lingerie, and hiking equipment of various sizes, types and conditions were recovered, but were not considered relevant to the search, since they appeared to be discarded or forgotten, and not torn off a human.

A small troop of Boy Scouts from the River Plaza section of Middletown New Jersey, searching alongside the banks of the Tohickon Creek, found a heavily damaged but still somewhat usable cell-phone with over $30 still remaining on a pre-paid plan. The discovery was considered significant by the search team because it was under a high vertical backdrop of sheer stone that was topped by a popular hiking trail called the *High Trail*, in contrast to the *Low Trail* that followed the creek. The team spent a long time sweeping both trails for any other clues, but in general the area was remarkably clean.

It was at this stage that I entered the picture. A car accident that summer had left me with a torn rotator cuff in my right shoulder, and I was still recovering from surgery and subsequent physical therapy. The local law-enforcement team was very capable, but lacked experience in following up on human remains, and I had some free time on my hands, so I was 'lent' to the case purely as an 'advisor', even though there was no reason for FBI involvement yet.

Well, I do not advise; I do.

Alex Kincaid

Over the years I'd seen many versions of Alex Kincaid, if that indeed was his real name. He had a deep Irish brogue all right, even though he'd grown up in Philadelphia, having been raised in an inner-city conclave of fiercely clannish Irish immigrants, both legal and illegal (Alex readily admittedly belonging to the latter).

Yes, I'd seen many versions of him, most turning out exactly as they appeared at first glance, vagrants of dubious origins who worked infrequently as day laborers, uprooting themselves on a whim, chasing the illusory dream of respectability, without doing anything worthy of the title.

I honestly did not know if that was his real name, and I had no real desire nor reason to turn over that rock, which would only serve to divert me from my true quest. *But hold it right there young lady*, some of you finicky readers may rightfully assert yourselves, and I acknowledge their propriety in questioning the validity of my judgment; *guilty as charged, so let's move right along, shall we?*

Forever an indigent, Alex had spent his young adulthood in Arizona, doing odd jobs, and had mastered living underneath the stars in formal campgrounds. *The federal ones are free*, he said, and Bucks County of Pennsylvania only charged its residents $12 per night, three less than the fare for non-residents, to stay overnight at Tohickon Valley.

He, his common law wife and five-year old son had just vacated an apartment in Doylestown, where their landlady had exchanged an extra month of shelter for painting the place, and they were now sleeping in his van at Tohickon Valley.

An examination of the cell phone discovered by the Scouts yielded some interesting information – although only a few inconsequential calls were made, all of them were outgoing. The integral camera had about a dozen pictures, some taken around Tohickon Valley. The general consensus was that the phone was damaged not by an animal, but due to having been thrown with considerable force, most likely from the *High Trail*, since it was found on the opposite bank of the creek.

Taken by itself, the act of tossing a cell phone did not necessarily point to foul play; after all, lives there one amongst us who has not been sorely tempted to do likewise? However, cell reception was fair throughout the region, given the rough terrain, and the phone had a decent charge still left on its battery, probably because it was not turned on. It was dusted for fingerprints, but the recoverable and usable ones did not match the national FBI database. The finger found in the cub – a middle finger - was too far deteriorated to extract any prints. The last activity on the phone ended at 4:44 pm on October 12th, the day before the cub's first sighting in the area.

A scan of the park ranger's logs turned up a family – the Kincaids - who had been residing in the camp for just under a month, and were still around, and a solitary camper who seemingly vanished one day.

"He drove up in a green Subaru station wagon," Alex said, his face lighting up with a smile that highlighted his white, even teeth. "He asked me if you needed a tent to sleep here. At first I thought that he was offering to give me a tent to use, since we had none," Alex said with a warm and sincere laugh, "but it dawned on me right away that what he was really asking was if *he* would get thrown out of the camp for sleeping in his car. I saw him for the last time on the eve of Columbus Day. I remember that because I had to get up by half past four the next morning at the latest to go to a job site. I'd just finished brushing my teeth and was taking off my socks and shoes before hopping in the shower," Alex said, explaining that he always showered in his clothes, to wash them at the same time. *"I use Tom's toothpaste too*, the stranger said, pointing to my stuff on the sink. I replied that it was my wife's new age stuff. When my wife met him, she got a nice, warm aura from him." She was a reluctant psychic, Alex said, and mostly gave shiatsu massages – for free. It was not like she allowed them to take off their clothes or some crazy stuff like that, he said.

It was interesting, I thought, that Alex used *stuff* instead of that other word people have a bad habit of using in its place. *Where were his wife and son*, I asked. Being Sunday, they were attending church. Alex admitted his disdain for organized religion, and volunteered that his prejudice in that particular regard also contributed to the normal marital stresses.

Alex's wife had wanted to invite the stranger over to join their campfire one night, he said, not that they had any solid food to offer, but just for companionship. "I never saw him cook anything, or even start a fire," said Alex, "but I think he mostly ate yogurt and bananas."

He was the only one at the campground who seemed to be alone, Alex said, and mostly he just sat in his car, rarely with the engine running.

"What was he doing – just sitting there?" I asked, interested in establishing a frame of mind.

"He was two sites away, and my eyesight isn't what it used to be," said Alex, "but he always sat in the passenger's seat up front, sometimes straight, sometimes reclined."

I had a pack of cheap Skydancer Native American cigarettes, ordered in bulk online at $23 a carton, with Lucky Strikes running a few pennies under $50 from the same vendor, shipping and handling always extra, of course – that's where the online retailers really made their profits. *If you are a Benson & Hedges cigarette smoker, Skydancer is what you want*, boasted the manufacturer's web site. Not that I smoked, and even if I did, I'd probably have stuck to Marlboro's, which I had tried quite unsuccessfully in a Missouri high school at my best friend's exhortations; I always carried them around to get people to talk. Alex gratefully lit one up, and since there were only a few left, I gave him the pack. Yes, I know, contributing to the spread of cancer and disease and all that, but I knew that most likely Alex was destined to die first of other causes than lung cancer. "Did he have the car running?"

Alex shook his head. Apparently he just sat there listening to AM radio. "I didn't see him smoke," said Alex, "and of course alcohol and drugs are prohibited in these campgrounds. He always waved when we passed each other. I don't know why he left without saying goodbye, even though we didn't really know each other."

But that last evening, said Alex, the stranger was with a very young man, but definitely not a boy. "It wasn't any of my business," he said, "but I don't think it was his son, and I never saw him before, and never again."

The young man was very well dressed in stylish hiking attire, and talked to the stranger out in the open in a normal manner for almost half an hour before heading alone towards the High Trail, passing the Kincaids' campsite without acknowledging them.

Alice Kincaid

That afternoon, I did a few things that were dreadfully imprudent and just plain wrong, some not for the first time in my life either, sad to admit.

"I'm not going to charge you anything," Alice Kincaid said after I had politely declined her unsolicited and unexpected offer for a massage. Besides, didn't Alex say that her massages were always on the house?

Nevertheless, something about Alice made me trust her, much against my training, indoctrination and ingrained natural instinct. Maybe it was that Alex had seeded my first opinions of his wife by accusing her of being a child in a grown woman's body, or maybe it was her cornflower blue eyes bounded by simple glasses set against a backdrop of clear skin and long, straight straw blond hair under an olive knit beanie, white shirt and blue jeans that could have just as easily adorned a freshman at Vassar or Yale.

But in Alice's specific case, her lack of formal education had undeniably ruled out all privileges enjoyed by the certifiably pedigreed. Also missing were the standard accoutrements such as the obligatory Cartier Tank watch and the patent leather Gucci loafers.

I readily confess that I should have kept my professional objectivity, but there was also the overwhelming realization that *but for the Grace of God go I.* I was not born with a silver spoon in my mouth either, but I had better control over my personal decisions, or so I thought. My right shoulder had started hurting again, and was screaming for some attention.

After she'd returned from church, Alex had taken their son Jason to see her parents, with whom she was strictly on non-speaking terms. It would not surprise me if that arrangement seemed a bit strange to you, but I have noticed that kind of largesse when I least expected it.

She'd swung open the rear doors to the long-wheelbase van, revealing, much to my astonishment, a bed made with military precision, a top sheet neatly drawn tight and crisply tucked around the corners. The pillows were neatly fluffed, but honestly, even with mints, they did not lead me to believe it was the Sheraton. Underneath, I could see that the rear deck had been lined with some sort of wood flooring shellacked an unnatural yellow.

I lay down on my stomach after removing my field jacket, and Alice worked on my right shoulder, left, neck and back, in that order. Her technique was debatable, but this was not costing me anything, and moreover it was saving me a trip to the physical therapist.

Fifteen minutes later, she made me roll over onto my back, and then proceeded to massage my neck. For a brief moment, I confess to experiencing unease as her warm, smooth hands circled my neck. His first name was Jack, she said, and that's all she knew. Yes, she had massaged him one Sunday. *Was this how she killed him?* My hands were clasped around my belly, and I very easily could have brought them straight up to break her light grip, so I just opened my eyes.

Most people react the same way, she said softly without stopping, her blonde hair like strands of pure gold in the afternoon sun that filtered through the trees. She did not wear any perfume at all; even her clothes carried no scent. The very slight trace of burnt oil and gasoline was of course due to the van and its mechanisms. I could see one shoulder through the open neck of her clean, un-ironed white shirt, sleeves rolled midway up her slender forearms, and she was not wearing a brassiere.

It was possible, I reasoned later that day, that either one or both of them may have killed him – *Jack* – but they had volunteered a lot of information that would only draw attention to them, and though they were indigent, they were not dumb. After all, they could have claimed to having no contact other than a passing, courteous hello. At this point, there was no lawful way to detain them, but I made a mental note to ask the local police to dig further. I knew that the Subaru wagon would have to be located for examination, but no one knew its license plate number, save that it was from Pennsylvania.

What had prompted her to give him a massage that Sunday, said Alice, was a small incident which took place between Jack and a younger camper. She'd witnessed the younger man, whom she had never seen before, throw a well-aimed stone at a large bird that flew repeatedly over him, flapping its wings and squawking loudly. Jack had quietly approached him with his hands tucked into the pockets of his windbreaker, and said that if the rangers saw him harassing the wildlife, they would ticket him.

Well, I ain't getting crapped on my head by a stupid bird, the young man had said, although with a choicer vocabulary, Alice told me with a smile.

After that, Jack repeated his warning, and added that the bird was probably trying to protect its brood, and that it had a God-given right to crap just about wherever it pleased; that had agitated the young man, who in turn had urged Jack to mind his own business, again in his own colorful vernacular.

Alice said that she had defused the situation by walking Jack away, since she did not want him to get hurt by the younger man, who had long, black unkempt hair and wore a tattered hunter's camouflage outfit, and carried a big hunting knife on his belt. She didn't even know if it was legal to do so.

I gave her ten bucks for the massage, which she accepted only with great reluctance, making me feel as though I had just debased an artist.

Upton Wallaby

The license plate in a photo, one of over a dozen retrieved off the cell phone, was too fuzzy to make out with the naked eye, until I enlisted a nice Indian techie named Ravi at the field office helped me out. I had once made the mistake of referring to him as *the IT guy*, only to be firmly and politely informed that he was a *software specialist*.

Ravi enhanced the picture on his computer, managing to get a couple of letters off it. That helped me identify its rightful owner as Mr. Upton Wallaby of New Hope, Pennsylvania. Fortunately for himself, Mr. Wallaby was eighty-five years old, mostly alive, and still in possession of all of his digits despite having fought for his country during the World War II and in Korea.

With long, brilliant white hair brushed back without a discernible part, a narrow, long face, and a lean, tall stature, Mr. Wallaby looked a lot like the Hollywood actor Richard Mulligan, right down to the muted tie and brown cardigan. Maybe he could not understand my Missouri accent, of which I am convinced only a shadow remains, or maybe he was a bit hard of hearing, I really don't know, but the mere act of introducing myself took over five minutes, and hardly thirty seconds later he had forgotten who I was, and the purpose of my paying him a visit.

Just as I was fishing around for my car keys, having given up all hope of learning anything, I heard a toilet flush upstairs, and an elderly lady – so full of beans compared to him - descended the stairs, drying her hands on her tidy apron. She gently held his chin and persistently tugged at it until he looked directly at her, and said, "I'm back, Upton."

"Where is my tea?" Mr. Wallaby asked me testily, his bushy white eyebrows raised.

"I'll get it for you," I said, hurriedly following the lady into the kitchen. "I'm sorry about your husband," I said. "It must be very difficult for you."

The lady stared at me crossly. "My husband's been dead over twenty years!" She was Mr. Wallaby's caregiver, although she used the phrase *baby sitter*. Rudely pointing a forefinger straight between my eyeballs, she said, "For heaven's sake, why didn't your agency explain all that to you before they sent you here? I begged them to not send a young, inexperienced person like you to waste my time! You probably have no experience whatsoever in caring for the elderly, do you now?"

I politely showed her my badge and explained that although I did work for an agency of sorts, I was not there in the capacity of a caregiver, after which her demeanor changed slightly for the worse; it was as if I had wrongfully taken away her right to berate me further. She was much older than me, and had understandably lived a difficult life, so I did not let her bother me too much.

"It's cold in here," Mr. Wallaby complained, standing directly in front of the heater when I went back to the living room to hand him his steaming hot Darjeeling tea, with milk and sugar. I thought Mr. Wallaby would surely have appreciated a nice cookie with his tea but the lady said that it would not be a good idea to mess with his daily routine, although it appeared to be part of hers.

The dial on the wall-mounted combination electric heater and air conditioner was all the way to the red, and I could hear the little motor running its heart out, but wheezing out only a mild puff of hot air. Poking around, I found the hatch for the filter and pulled it out, finding it solidly blocked by a foul blanket of long, brittle wispy human hair and other detritus, short stubby animal hair, dark dust bunnies, and general brown fuzz, smelling sickeningly of very stale cigarette smoke. Cleaning out the filter helped somewhat, but the front grill was also quite clogged.

The vacuum cleaner was an old upright that did not have a detachable wand, so I asked the lady for some paper towels, Windex and Q-Tips, only to have her grudgingly give me a wrinkled paper napkin from Dunkin Donuts, and a solitary Q-Tip. I bet you dollars to donuts that she probably pocketed a few of his supplies, if you know what I mean. Cleaning out the ventilation grill took me an hour, and by then he had long forgotten that he was cold, but Mr. Wallaby finally had some heat.

I left Mr. Upton Wallaby with only scant more information than when I had met him, and all of it had come from his caregiver, none from him; his only grandson had used the Subaru wagon through high school, until he lost his life serving in Afghanistan, and the car was literally given away, license plates and all. There was no record of who had it, but the lady guessed that he was in his forties, and seemed a little shop-worn, which was remarkable coming from her, but that was about all that she could remember, given that she had started taking care of Mr. Wallaby at just around that time.

There was no record of the transaction that had occurred over two months prior, so the car was still in Mr. Wallaby's name, as was the insurance. I jotted down in my notebook to have the Pennsylvania Department of Social Services look into his affairs.

Then, I hit the jackpot – a police officer in Red Bank, New Jersey, had flagged the old Subaru on River Road for having an expired inspection sticker, and had issued a ticket to a Jack Mulroney of Sea Bright, New Jersey.

Anita Bansfield

Wednesday October 29, 9:00 a.m., Red Bank, New Jersey

"He came to the window just as I had opened the door to go to the ladies' room," said Anita Bansfield, behind the counter at the Red Bank courthouse. "Hardly before I had finished asking him if I could help him, he just went to pieces! Tapping fretfully on his passport, he kept saying *I am a US citizen, I am unemployed, divorced, and I cannot afford to pay this ticket that I got for driving an old car with an expired inspection sticker!*"

"What did you do then," I asked.

She had rubbed his shoulder and patted his back, said Anita. He was not angry, before or afterwards, but very contrite. This was her thirty-fifth year working for Red Bank, Anita declared, although she had seen plenty of people visibly and vocally angry at having to pay for violations, rarely had she ever run into someone sobbing fitfully in abject embarrassment and shame at not being able to pay a fine.

She went into the computer system, she said, and gave him another thirty days to come up with the money, and wrote down her name and phone number, with specific instructions for him to call if he needed more time. "There's no reason for a person to have to deal with that amount of stress," she said.

To be blunt, I had no idea that I would be unearthing these nuggets of information before I set foot in that building. What had piqued my interest in making that trip to the courthouse was that not only had the ticket not been paid on time, but had received not one, but two extensions. That does not happen frequently. More importantly, I discovered that Jack Mulroney had been divorced. Now I was cooking with gas.

Ruthie Clearwater

If you have never been on a genuine drawbridge, you'd better find one real quick, because just like genuine stainless-steel diners and drive-in movie theaters that brightened the New Jersey of yore, they too are rapidly disappearing from our landscape.

The Rumson drawbridge, formally known as the Rumson Sea Bright Bridge, connecting tony Rumson to tiny Sea Bright is losing its sister, the Highlands drawbridge, to a fixed and higher, broad-sweeping, modern arc of steel reinforced concrete on spindly piers. Progress has its advantages, I suppose, but as I waited patiently for the bridge keeper to lower the Rumson drawbridge, raised to allow a single small sailboat to pass, I had to sadly accept that this was a relic of America past.

The traffic light at the bottom of the bridge, where it met Ocean Avenue, also called Route 36, turned red, leaving me straddling both of the grated sections that Id seen swing well up hardly a minute ago. Through a serrated gap of about an inch between the two plates, I could see the rapid waters of the Shrewsbury River rush between the massive footings. Moving traffic on the opposing lane caused the two halves to vibrate up and down quite disconcertingly, and I was able to breathe freely again only after reaching fixed tarmac.

I'd spoken with Ruthie Clearwater briefly on the phone, and had detected a slight Midwestern drawl. I learned a long ago not to ask too many questions on the phone, but to keep the conversation short. If I do all the questioning face to face, I can watch their reactions and gestures. Many people lie with words, but their body language usually tells the real story.

As luck would have it, Ruthie had been born and raised in rural Springfield, Missouri. She had come to Sea Bright via San Diego, where she met her husband, a Coast Guard enlistee. Eventually he was assigned to the Mid-Atlantic seaboard, and she found work as a math teacher at the Holy Cross Catholic School in neighboring Rumson. I remembered driving past that church just before the bridge.

In the late 1980s, the Clearwaters had purchased an apartment in a riverfront motel going into bankruptcy, which they had recently started renting out to summer vacationers, mostly regulars, who invariably reserved their slot well in advance on a weekly basis. From a week after

Labor Day to a fortnight prior to the next Memorial Day, they listed it as a winter rental, for a very reasonable monthly rate.

"The condo association pays for the gas," said Ruthie as she met me at the ground-floor apartment, "which runs the hot water, and also feeds the gas stove here. The electric is in my name, and I am on a monthly budget plan, so I charge an extra $100 per month for that, and settle it out with the tenant before the final month."

Ruthie squinted at the sketch before confirming that it was the person she knew as Jack Mulroney, but did not think that the photo from the driver's license resembled him much at all, and I couldn't blame her, as that photo was at least a dozen years old. To my trained eye, however, the similarities between the composite that we had created from the Kincaids' descriptions picked out many of his features quite accurately, adjusted for age.

The past summer had been rough, primarily due to the poor economy, she said, and none of their normal tenants had made any commitments. So they had put it up for winter rental at the end of June.

She had taken a goat-cheese sandwich with roasted peppers and arugula, purchased at the whimsically named cafe *The Flaky Tart*, to the apartment, meaning to enjoy a nice lunch after hanging up a *For Rent* sign on the front door. "Less than a minute later he is at the door," she said, "saying that he would take it if it was still available."

"Did you run a credit check on him?"

"No. You must understand, usually the winter renters here can barely pony up the first rent check, let alone the deposit. You have no idea how many ask me to just hold on to the deposit check, and not cash it, so when he gave me cash to cover both, that was enough of a credit check for me."

"You weren't afraid that maybe it was drug money or something?"

She laughed. "If you saw him, that notion would never cross your mind, believe me."

It was a small but comfortable one-bedroom apartment. There was a sliding glass door that opened out onto a common green, and beyond that lay the Shrewsbury river, kept at bay by a bulkhead.

The water was eerily glassy, and Ruthie rolled her eyes when I commented on that. "That's only because it's slack tide," she said. "The direction of the current changes with the high and low tides, and the water runs fiercely fast and turbulent." Although there were only a couple of small power boats puttering around, Ruthie said that during warmer days the waterway got quite crowded.

"Do you fish off the bulkhead?"

Ruthie made a face. "We did until a couple of years ago."

Then some young teenaged girl had complained to her condo association about the horrors she had witnessed, with the tenants killing the cute fishies, beheading them, gutting them to throw their bloody entrails back into the river and so on an so forth. "That put an end to the fishing from our property here," Ruthie said, "which is a pity, because the sea bass and blues run by here."

Thankfully, she said, one could still fish off the drawbridge where it was technically prohibited, but the operators let them be, or at the public beach, if one was not fortunate enough to know someone with a small boat.

"It's a shame that the association had decided to prohibit fishing here," she said, "but we all have to learn to live together, or lose everything." I was quite sure that she was commenting on the girl, and not the neighbors, but either way it made sense.

The bedroom was outfitted with a full-size bed, with a trundle bed normally tucked away underneath it, which could be pulled out as needed. The couch in the main room converted into a sleeper, she said, and that was where Jack Mulroney slept, so that he could enjoy the views.

"I thought that this might help," she said, giving me a copy of his lease. Although the lease did not record his Social Security number, the phone number lightly scribbled at the bottom under his signature was most gratifying, since it matched the number of the cell phone retrieved by the Boy Scouts.

You see, I really had no interest in starting with his birth and tracking every single thing he'd ever done in his life, but I wanted to start with the present and work my way back to look at stuff that he may have done that contributed to his demise. Unfortunately for me, he had paid his rent by cash, always punctually, and had not subscribed to any utility like a telephone land line, cable or satellite television. He did not even have a bank account; he had no loans, debts, credit cards or other obligations; he had no visible footprint to speak of in our modern society that is so bent on full disclosure and extensive records.

Although I could have searched for every Mulroney, keep in mind that Jack may have been his nickname, so I would have to search for John also, and that would just turn up too many people, each of whom I would have to track. All J. Mulroneys appeared to be accounted for, since no one by that name had been specifically reported as missing. But disturbingly, I could not find a suitable match based on his birth date, from his driver's license.

"What did he do for a living?" I asked.

"I didn't ask him that, and he did not volunteer it," she said tightly. "His money was as green as anyone else's, and he was always punctual," she said, clearly proud of her choice in picking him as a dependable tenant, and in her way of not violating a tenant's privacy. But of course, that did not help me out.

"He washed his clothes," said Ruthie. Didn't we all, I thought. "He washed them by hand, in a pail, and draped them over a collapsible drying rack in the tub. He really didn't have enough clothes to fill the washer that is available to all the residents."

Sea Bright was a time-warp surrounded by some of the finest estates in the country. It was basically a thin strip of sand dunes with million-dollar views, separated from Rumson by the Shrewsbury river, and from the Atlantic ocean by a seawall. A good chunk of the seashore was taken up by *beach club row*, which had members going back three generations, and open only from Memorial Day through Labor Day, but fingers of public pathways poked through, allowing locals unfettered access to the steel-blue waters, fine sand and all the striped bass, flounder and bluefish they could catch by surf-fishing.

"Did Jack fish?"

"Well, he did ask where he could get good bait, and I sent him to Tom Giglio's bait shop. I think I saw him once heading towards the beach with a pole and a cooler... but who knows what was in the cooler," she laughed. "My husband always packs a six pack and a sandwich when he goes fishing, and he never once came back with any fish to fry, come to think about it!"

What an interesting place, I mused, where a transient could easily and acceptably stay anonymously in the shadows, whilst surrounded by the normally very suspicious wealthy. But the local economy was completely reliant on seasonal visitors, most of whom had summer homes, and on year-round residents from Rumson and Monmouth Beach, who commuted to work on a high-speed ferry service that dropped them off on Manhattan's Wall Street in under an hour.

"It is brutal," said Ruthie, "to be unemployed this year. I don't see any end in sight, so you?"

In the summer, the beach clubs employed college students to be lifeguards, cooks, waitresses and janitors. With the economy in trouble, no one was spending money on home improvements, and instead were looking to just sell and get out, if the plentiful *For Sale* signs on many homes were any indication.

None of his neighbors had lodged any complaint against him, said Ruthie, and he himself had not said anything about his neighbors; that was not to say everything was hunky-dory between all of the other neighbors, she admitted readily, but somehow he steered clear of getting involved in any part of the normal frictions amongst people. He had seemed calm and considerate, and if she had to pick a single fault, it was that he had been aloof almost to the point of being rude.

One thing that she had noticed about him was that he had painfully scant possessions; *it was almost as if he lived out of a tin cup*, said Ruthie, so most definitely the fully furnished apartment had to have come in handy for Jack.

He did not do drugs, alcohol or cigarettes. *I wish all of the tenants were like him*, said Ruthie wistfully. Then one day late in September, he had called, only saying that he was leaving at the end of the month, and with that he had just melded back into the void. It certainly didn't seem as if he was on the lam from the law or anyone else, otherwise he wouldn't have bothered to give Ruthie notice.

Ruthie was a parishioner of Holy Cross, and she did not recall ever seeing him there; but there was the historic St. George's-By-The-River Episcopal Church across the river in Rumson, and the United Methodist Church in Sea Bright. Had Jack Mulroney had attended either one, and if so, had he sought the help and counsel of their clergy?

Leaving Ruthie, who jokingly said that she would not leave town without informing me, I walked towards the bridge, passing a tiny, well-maintained parcel of land called the Swing Bridge Park. The drawbridge was built in 1952, right next to an old Swing Bridge, which in turn had dated back to 1901. The subsequent tear-down of the older bridge had divided Rumson Road into two pieces, isolating a tiny vestigial section of just two addresses in Sea bright.

I walked over to the Sea Bright post office, where the counter, which was only open from 9:00 a.m. to noon, was about to close. "We are just an outpost of the Rumson post office," said the clerk. "Jack Mulroney? He's one of my best customers," she said with a loud guffaw, after I gave her his address. "Never saw him, never had to deliver a single piece of mail with his name on it!"

The Flaky Tart

It was noon, and I hadn't eaten at all that morning, so I stopped by the Flaky Tart for lunch, at Ruthie's strong recommendation.

Marie Jackson poured two large bowls of chili served with creme fraiche and red onions, my favorite, one for me, and another for herself, as we talked. Much to my surprise, she knew Jack.

"Often he walked past my shop," said Marie, "always wearing faded jeans, a blue windbreaker and a fisherman's cap. But he never did come in." The Flaky Tart looked very elegant, due to the marbled floor, polished wood furniture, rows of coffee urns, and mouth-watering assortments of heavenly pastries, including the namesake tarts, which belied its reasonable prices.

"We are open only until 5pm, and bake everything fresh each morning," said Marie, "and I started putting out loaves of bread for 50 cents each at the end of the day. He saw the sign, came in one day, tried one, and liked it."

But that hadn't been the end of their relationship, Marie

said, pointing to a large white sign on the counter, which read:

Please inquire about our school lunch program

"The local schools don't serve lunch to the kids," said Marie, "and one day a mother asked if we delivered our sandwiches, soups and muffins to her kids at school." So that was exactly what Marie started doing, initially as an experiment. It worked out very well all around until right after Labor Day, when she lost a delivery girl to the Fall semester at Brookdale Community College.

"I casually mentioned that I was looking for a reliable delivery person, and he seemed interested. We chatted sometime around the middle of September," said Marie. "Funny thing is that I ladled a bowl of soup for him as we talked, and he would not accept it unless I allowed him to pay for it. Some people are like that."

He had asked a few questions about the whole process that Marie had in place, from taking the orders to confirming back to the parent that the food had been successfully delivered in a timely fashion to the child, so he was definitely interested.

But that was the last time Marie saw him. "I am pretty sure that he could have used the money. I don't know his story, but I think he was a decent guy who had simply fallen on hard times."

I thanked Marie for her soup and a slice of heavenly carrot cake that had followed, but she wouldn't accept payment.

"I hope that he is OK. He certainly ate a lot of onions," she said.

Pastor Owen Pears

Wednesday October 29, 3:30 p.m., United Methodist Church, Sea Bright, New Jersey

"We are here whenever a man needs help in opening himself to God," said Pastor Owen Pears. "Often a troubled soul cannot see that of course God always welcomes those who seek Him, no applications get rejected there." As the daughter of a Methodist Minister, I know that's so true. Outside Pastor Owen's church was a small fountain, and a sign that read:

> *Toss a coin,*
> *Say a prayer,*
> *Look up,*
> *Jesus is there.*

Jack Mulroney had attended Sunday Service sporadically, and seemed reserved, "But he knew that he was always welcome here," said Pastor Owen, as he preferred to be called.

The original church, built in 1889, had succumbed to a fire in 1891 that had destroyed most of Sea Bright. A year later, it had been rebuilt, and over the ensuing decades, various capital projects had been undertaken to keep up with the fierce storms of the Atlantic that regularly ravaged this precarious sandbar and its buildings and denizens.

The church had a small congregation, meeting every Sunday morning at 9:30 for service. Afterwards, a small meal was served, and the parishioners would sit down at a long table to eat, find out how everyone was doing, and serve cake to celebrate birthdays. But even when he did show up for the service, Jack never stayed for the food.

When I asked him if Jack ever seemed to be depressed or suicidal, Pastor Owen said that he really didn't know, since Jack had never taken him into his confidence. A local chapter of Alcoholics Anonymous met regularly in the basement of the church, and the AA's point was that, first you had to admit that you had a problem, and then seek help. That was a big problem for most, as I knew so well personally.

"It's easy to probe a young adolescent, but it's another thing to intrude into a grown person's life. To encourage openness, we always pray as a group for the Lord to take care of each other's problems, and we always thank the Lord," said Pastor Owen. On a personal level, he spoke of a young Lizzie who got up one day at the end of the service and thanked God for a precious, solitary gallon of gasoline that He had put in her car.

Sadly, I could match every tale like that, which I had not only heard, but had experienced myself. I knew such days long ago when one bitter night the bank's ATM would not let me take out two out of the $9 I thought I had in my account, to buy a bag of yellow onions that would keep me going for at least for a week as the main and often only course.

There are a lot of people who would think *Tobacco Road* is a chronicle of the lifestyles of the rich and famous.

Where the Blues Run

Wednesday October 29, 5:30 p.m., Giglio's Bait and Tackle, Sea Bright, New Jersey

Tom Giglio's Bait and Tackle was across the street from the Methodist church, so I dropped by. "Jack was a very reluctant fisherman," said Tom, "who most certainly did not enjoy fishing even one tiny bit. He was the most squeamish guy I ever ran into, and I think he fished only to feed himself. Do you fish?"

I certainly knew how to fish the streams, rivers and lakes of Missouri and Pennsylvania, and had spent many a pleasant dawn in fruitful pursuit of pretty rainbow trout and ugly catfish, both of which made for good eating in their own ways, but had never spent much time near an ocean to pursue saltwater fish. In fact, I remember one occasion when I suggested borrowing a row boat and heading out on the Lake of the Ozarks to fish. On a first date. I don't know if I scared him away, but his interest in me had waned rapidly after that.

"This is a paradise for bluefish and striped bass," said Tom, himself a third-generation owner of the shop established in 1961. "Many are sport-fishermen," he said, "but that's also where a few catch their breakfast, lunch and dinner."

I thought that blues were oily and generally yucky to eat, but Tom corrected me, explaining that their oiliness was what caused the fish to decay quite rapidly after being caught. "Fillet them right there, ice them right away, and keep them away from fresh water - *that's* the secret to a great bluefish dinner. That's why you see fishermen carry large coolers here."

Another way, although quite messy, was to bleed them in a particular way that did not sound appetizing.

"You got to be careful when fishing blues, and watch your leaders - they better be steel - and your fingers - they better be out of the blue's mouth!" That was how he had originally met Jack. "He came in with a bandaged pinky, and wanted to know how to steer clear of blues and land the stripers."

Blues are generally great fighters, Tom said, and are such voracious eaters, even resorting to cannibalism, that it was very easy to catch them. So he shared a few recipes and techniques with Jack.

"Did he have a boat?"

"No, and that's unfortunate," said Tom. "You should see the boats, big and small, drifting rapidly up and down the river with the tide, sometimes even sideways, their engines idling. They start south in Monmouth Beach, and generally turn around before the Rumson bridge, and keep doing it all day, when the blues run."

The blues ran in schools, and were such messy eaters that it was as if they created their own chum, so all one had to do was watch the gulls to know exactly where they were.

It was a bit more difficult to catch them by surf-fishing, especially standing high and dry on the shore. "You got to get past the shallow shelf to deeper water using waders," said Tom. The frequent storms ate away at the soft sand, creating a shallow shelf, generally avoided by large fish, that extended almost a couple of hundred feet into the ocean.

Jack had looked longingly at the waders, but seemed reluctant to invest in them, said Tom, so had ended up returning empty handed most days.

"I wanted to help him out, and one day I had a guy return a great pair that his girlfriend had bought for him somewhere else, but he said that they were just the wrong color, so he had worn them a couple of times to humor her and finally dropped them off here. So I offered them to Jack for free."

I had a hunch that Jack did not accept them for free, and I was right. "So I struck a deal with him," said Tom, "that he would come in and clean out my freezers three times in exchange."

He smiled, "Truthfully I said *thrice* just to make him feel that I was not doing this for charity."

The Software Specialist known only as Ravi

Thursday October 30, 11:00 a.m., Doylestown, Pennsylvania

Ravi does have a last name, but it has so many consonants and syllables inharmoniously arranged that it seemed like his parents had poured a few handfuls of Scrabble letters on the table and called the ensuing mess a name. I cannot begin to tell you what it even sounds like. His is the last name that will not fit on most application forms, and I remember him telling me that his bank had chopped off his name to fit on the debit card.

Even Ravi had no clue as to what it meant, or at least that was what he claimed. Believe me, no one else in the USA seemed to have that last name, though for all I knew it was as common in India as Patel is in Edison, NJ.

"Ever used *Flickr*?" he asked, hardly able to contain his glee.

No, I had not, I readily confessed. Wasn't it an Internet database of movies or something?

47

"No, you're thinking of *imdb*," he said, with a dirty look that he probably reserved only for someone who ate with his left hand. "*Flickr* lets you upload your photos online, and share them with others."

I knew better than to lay out my abject ignorance on this, so I quietly wheeled my chair over to his side of the desk so that I could see the screen of his Apple computer. Besides, I could shoot a gun very well, and Ravi didn't know a heel from a muzzle flash.

"This is the last photo that we got off his cell phone," said Ravi, "which I uploaded to my *Flickr* account." He clicked something here and something there, and a window popped up, mostly blank. "If this photo had been taken with an *iPhone*, it would have all sorts of information such as the shutter speed, aperture, the exact geographic location where the photo was taken and all that," he said.

But since Mr. Mulroney only had had a cheap prepaid cell phone with a feeble camera, we had no such luck. "But we know exactly where in Tohickon Park that picture was taken, so I entered that information into *Flickr*."

A couple of mouse clicks later, a map appeared on his screen, with a red star. Now, I kid you not, this is what apparently exists in life as we speak, so bear with me as I try to explain what I saw. With a few more sleights of hand with that omnipotent mouse, he brought up thirty more stars on that map. "All these photos were taken by others within a ½ mile radius of Mulroney's photo, and within plus or minus 3 days of when we think that was taken, and uploaded to *Flickr*."

I told him that it was very nice, and that I was sure a bunch of smart geeks had done a great job in writing all that software, but also that I had absolutely no clue as to what it all meant. Zip. Zilch. Nada. Not a solitary clue.

"I looked at other pictures submitted by each person who took these," Ravi said, running his fingers through his hair, which meant that he was truly excited by what he was doing. "Look at this album," he whispered, almost as if he was afraid that the owner of that online album would flee upon hearing his name being mentioned.

I almost fell off my chair when I saw a high-resolution picture of the Subaru wagon, all glorious 13.5 mega-pixels of it, the license plate clearly visible with the naked eye. I could also make out that the inspection sticker in the lower corner of the windshield had expired in March.

"These, and a few other pictures in this guy's account," said Ravi, "were taken by a Nikon Coolpix 6000 digital camera with built-in GPS."

We found out online that the camera cost around $600 new. Ravi showed me another map, showing distinct clusters where pictures were taken with that camera, spanning about three weeks. Did these document Mr. Mulroney's last few weeks, I wanted to know.

With Ravi's help, we managed to identify and locate Mark Shepard, of Doylestown, PA, as the owner of that account. Let me tell you, in real life Mark Shepard turned out to be as innocuous as his name sounded. Even Ravi had predicted so, but I had to check him out.

He was about 22, 5'5", of slight build and probably weighed 130 pounds soaking wet and carrying a set of barbells. When he met me at his tastefully appointed condo, he was wearing a light green fleece pullover that complemented his short blonde hair, blue eyes and very fair, unblemished skin. Denim jeans and Penny loafers rounded out his attire.

Late that Sunday afternoon of October 19, he had been on one of his frequent hikes in Tohickon, he said, which had become more frequent since getting dumped by his long-time partner. Mark didn't know his name, he said, but had literally bumped into Jack at an overlook.

"I really thought that he was a jumper," said Mark, his puppy-dog eyes growing round; of course, he was not thinking of a *base jumper*, he added, instead crouching to imitate a swimmer diving off a board, while making a face.

"What led you to think that," I asked, stifling a smile.

"Once upon a time I had thought of jumping from there if my partner ever left me," said Mark as a matter-of-fact, his eyebrows narrowing, "but I am glad that I didn't. Nothing is ever worth doing that," he said softly.

No, it most certainly isn't, I agreed, wondering who could ever hurt somebody like him.

"He gave me his camera," said Mark, "when I told him that my partner had refused to return my Nikon after our breakup. "He said that he did not need it anymore, and he looked so disoriented and deflated that I really thought that he was going to jump."

Mark retrieved the small Coolpix camera from another room and handed it to me. "I asked him which way he was going, and was momentarily afraid that he was going to say *down*, you know?"

So gentle Mark Shepard, his own young little heart heavy with his own big burden, had walked Jack Mulroney back to the camp. Sometimes, great surprises do come in small, unassuming packages.

Myrtle Coughlin

Monday November 1, 1:30 p.m., Acme SavOn grocery store, Little Egg Harbor Township, New Jersey

I learned that as a baby name *Myrtle* certainly did not make the top 1,000 in 2009, but made it to #67 in 1919, and rapidly declined to #997 in 1964. If you don't believe me, look it up on www.ssa.gov/OACT/babynames, which is a fascinating site that is run by the Social Security Administration. In case you don't know it, I get my paycheck from the Federal Government, so I better plug it. When you see Myrtle, make sure that you pronounce her last name correctly, sounding out the *g*, but neither the *u* nor the *h*.

I think that Myrtle is a pleasant name, but it also rhymes so well with turtle, amongst others. School kids can be mean and vicious.

Myrtle was thirty, if that, very pregnant, and had a bad case of acne, which she did not fret about at all, smiling unabashedly in the photograph. "Yes, I remember that," she said, her eyes twinkling. "He came in very early one morning, when I was working the cash register," she said. "He wanted to know if we sold coffee by the cup. We do, but it's kind of in a strange place, so being as there were not many customers, I walked him up to it," she said. "I apologized for waddling like a duck, but he said that I should never say that again, but always be proud of being pregnant," said Myrtle. "He said that I looked beautiful, and to prove it he pulled a camera out of his pocket and snapped that picture."

"Did he say that he was going to email you that picture?" I asked, suddenly very hopeful.

Myrtle nodded. "But I didn't want to give a stranger, nice though he was, my email address, you know?" That was very prudent of her. "He had about ten cups of yogurt, which was on sale for 50 cents apiece," she said. "He wanted to know if it would keep without refrigeration for a couple of days at least."

That was a great price, I thought. However, Myrtle did not know if it was safe to eat unrefrigerated yogurt, but he said that he would take a chance on it. I had taken yogurt, to eat with raw cashew nuts and cereal on two-day hikes, and it remained edible if kept in a backpack away from heat, unlike cheese which just turned suspiciously soft.

"He came back later that evening for another cup of coffee," she said with a giggle, remembering another anecdote about him. "I think Julia was the clerk, and I buzzed her on the intercom to tell him that he had met his daily limit of two cups of coffee."

I glanced quickly to see if she had a ring on her finger, but she did not; then again, not every significant other is significant enough in life to get past having to cope with the barest of essentials, let alone invest in a woman's best friend. Believe me, I had grown up in exactly that kind of dire straits as a minister's daughter; show me a rich preacher and I'll show you a charlatan.

"I didn't know if I was to keep your coming here to ask me all these questions a secret," said Myrtle nervously, "but after you called, I did share your interest in that man with some of my friends."

"Oh?"

"Sam works at the Radio Shack next door, and he said that the guy bought an electric air compressor for twenty bucks, the kind that you plug into the cigarette lighter, and you can put air in your tires, even though it takes forever, you know? Sam remembered it because he had just received a shipment that very morning."

"Thanks, that helps," I lied. It wasn't as if he had bought a gun or hemlock. Then Myrtle said that he had also wanted a can of the stuff to inflate a flat tire, and had asked her if those things worked, which she did not know. The only garage in town closed early, she said. He had also bought a screwdriver after asking if he could return it if it was unused.

"Then there's Mitch who works at the Sleepy's store, and he said that the guy came in one night asking for a large plastic bag. Mitch asked him if he had a broken window, but the guy said that he was camping and needed something to place under his sleeping bag. But if he had a bag, why would he need a plastic sheet under it?"

"That's very interesting," I said, truthfully this time around. "Did he say where he was camping, do you know?" Of course I had already seen the pictures that he had taken – rather, the pictures that had been taken on that impressive little camera – and could pinpoint the geographic whereabouts to within mere feet, but it never hurts to get independent, corroborative supporting evidence. It would also help to know if he lied to others.

"At Bass River, where everyone comes to camp," said Myrtle. "That's a very popular campground. In fact, I remember the guy also bought a fake fireplace log here – you know, the one that's kind of expensive and comes in a pretty wrapper, and it's made of wax and sawdust or something? I was at the courtesy desk that time, and it was strange, but he actually wanted to *buy* a box of matches. I just gave him some for free. I guess he did not smoke, which *I* shouldn't really be doing either, my doctor says – I tried to quit a few times, but it's hard when everyone around you lights up and smokes like a chimney. It would be different if there's something else to do around here to pass the time." She grimaced, and paused to rub her belly. "The baby's really active, which means it will probably be a boy, I hope," she said.

Park Ranger Davis Mays

Monday November 3, 4:00 p.m., Bass River State Forest, Tuckerton, New Jersey

Ranger Davis Mays laughed heartily, and not at all derisively.

"He confessed that he was quite a chicken, and he sincerely doubted his ability to last through his first night here. After Labor Day, things get very quiet on weekdays, and picks up during the fall weekends, but with the rain that we've been getting, we had a lot of cancellations. It's been a bit desolate, as he correctly called it. Well, for a few nights he was the only camper and we have room for hundreds!"

He waved a hand dismissively. "I said if he got into trouble, all he had to do was call 911 if he had a cell phone, and a ranger would arrive within minutes. This is, after all, still New Jersey not the wilds of Alaska, though the cell reception is pretty bad in some parts." He pulled out his phone and showed me five bars. "But if I step outside and stand under those power lines, I get no bars."

He got up and gave me a small map of the area. "We got Lake Absegami here, and three major sites – the North Shore, the South Shore and the Group Camping area.

We're open year round." Reaching for his cap, he invited me along on a ride in his truck, white with green markings. "I need to make my run anyway, so I might as well give you the grand tour."

"We have big cabins that go for $55 a night," he said, "to sleep eight, but I've heard stories of far more teens pouring into one. They have full electric, and have the comforts of home, if your home has bunk beds."

Then they had *Shelters*, costing $40 a night, which slept four in bunk beds, but had no power, and no running water or toilets. "They use waterless toilets that serve three shelters each, or they can walk a short way to use a full, heated bathroom with nice, hot showers, flush toilets and even hand dryers. We even have power to run those electric razors and things."

The cabins and the shelters were restricted to the North Shore, and we were headed towards the South Shore.

We were on a narrow, paved road that followed the shores of Lake Absegami, which I glimpsed through breaks in the scrappy pine trees that gave the region its nickname of Pinelands, whose inhabitants were referred to as *Pineys*, which was either considered a badge of honor or an outright insult, depending on who uttered it.

A quarter of a mile up, he turned around into a 1-way road that ran parallel to the main drag, and stopped in front of the full, heated bathroom. There was even a small but well-maintained self-service Laundromat with two washers and two dryers that ran for $1.50 each, but you had to bring your own supplies.

"We send the folks down to the Acme," he said, "it's only five miles from here if you turn left on Stage Road and make a right at the first flashing light. There's also a McDonald's there."

Surprisingly, the ground was mostly hard sand covered by pine needles. "It's pretty noisy with the sound of those trucks," I said, having to speak a bit louder due to the brisk wind.

The ranger shook his head, pointing his hand up towards the clear, deep blue sky. "It's them Air National Guard A-10 Warthogs and F-16 jets upstairs practicing their bombing runs."

Apparently Bass River State Forest had the Warren Grove Air-to-Ground gunnery range as its neighbors. He took me down a narrow path that led to the lake, and we stood in a clearing hardly large enough for one person, with the waters lapping at our feet. He had work boots on, and I had flats that were completely soaked through, but I remained stoic and said nothing.

Overhead, a continuous parade of fighter jets played out an eerie, tightly choreographed aerial drama that started with the aircraft diving from about 1,000 feet over the lake, and banking vertically over a covered bathing pavilion that separated the North Shore from the South, turning tightly while still losing altitude like dropped rocks, and sounding like trucks downshifting to hurriedly bleed off speed. By the time they straightened out, they disappeared from sight, skimming the low treetops, and eventually screamed off under full power, as the next fighter plummeted into its assigned slot in the ballet.

We crossed the road and stopped at one of the campsites. "This is where he parked his car for quite a few nights, pointed towards the bathrooms." said the ranger. "At night these stay well lit for safety, and most people complain that the lights are too bright, but I guess when you're alone…"

"He didn't have a tent?"

"I asked him that, and he said that even if he had, he would still prefer to sleep in the car, with it being quite cool and all. But mostly I think, like he said, he was chicken." He stopped abruptly, and apologized for casting judgment. "It can be spooky here without anyone around, even when you are wide awake." He smiled briefly, "I could tell you about the famous Pinelands Jersey Devil, but maybe some other time."

The ranger had asked him if he carried any weapons, which were strictly prohibited. The only thing in his car even remotely resembling a weapon was a screwdriver, he had replied, especially since he was missing the jack and the lug wrench.

Each campsite, costing $20 a night, had a wooden picnic table with attached benches, and a fire-pit consisting of a band of weathered iron with an adjustable grate over one side. "Where do they get firewood?"

"Of course we don't allow cutting down any trees, but they are welcome to use any downed branches and fallen twigs. Back at the ranger station we sell large bags of kiln-dried wood already cut up to the right size, and they even come with fire starters. I use them myself, and they work out real good."

"Did you ever see someone with a Duraflame log?"

"The short answer is *No*, but I guess it takes all kinds." He mulled that for a few seconds. "I'd prefer that over the dim bulbs that use gasoline, aerosol hair sprays, bug repellent, cooking oil, salad dressing lighter fluid, Styrofoam plates, t-shirts, what have you. – I think that I have seen it all, though. Many use newspapers, which works well, but causes small wisps of burning embers to waft up in the breeze, and can come down elsewhere and start a wildfire. I don't recommend that at all, but the other stuff can easily hurt you real bad or even kill you."

There were a few pieces of wood lying around, charred on one side only, having been too big to burn. There were lots of smaller branches and twigs with which I could have easily started a decent fire and stayed warm for a whole evening, but then again I am good at that kind of thing, having backpacked in high country.

Jack Mulroney had spent about a week at that particular site, #67. "He renewed it every day, and specifically asked for it," said the ranger. That last Friday and Saturday he had selected a *Lean-To*, which went for $30 a night, and in spite of its name, was fully enclosed.

The one he had rented, #6, was the one closest to the lake, although it did not have a view of it, with its row of windows looking out into the woods. It had a slanted roof that was at its highest over the windows, and came down to about four feet at the other end. The only door was at one side, and upon entering, there was a cast iron stove mounted over a stone hearth on the opposite side.

The wood itself was dark, probably with the patina of smoke

and age, and with the overhead canopy of trees, little light illuminated the room even on that sunny afternoon.

"I remember that weekend all the Lean-Tos were rented out. We had cabins that were available, but we also had many late cancellations as the day progressed, due to that brisk Nor'easter brewing."

He specifically asked for that unit. "Most of our campers are regulars," said the ranger, "and always ask for particular ones. Many think of them as *their* units, and they end up taking better care of them, though a few try to make minor modifications, which we strictly prohibit. I guess it all evens out in the end."

"Was he a regular, then?"

"No, as far as I know I had never seen him before that small stretch. I'm not here all the time, though; we operate in shifts."

I used a small flashlight, trying to spot anything of value, but there were no discernible carvings in the wood, or spray-painted statements of adoration. For a shack in the woods operated on the basis of daily rentals, it was surprisingly clean.

We went up to the lake, and I spent a few minutes looking around, captivated by the ethereal, haunting beauty of the lake, with disturbing and distracting images of that movie Friday the 13th coming to mind. Behind us, there was a large pavilion with open sides, dwarfing the solitary wooden picnic table in the center.

He did not have any run-ins with the staff or other campers, and had pretty much kept to himself. Other than a call or two to the ranger station, made during daylight hours, he had not used his cell phone, but had taken a few pictures around the park, all of it scenery, with absolutely no people at all, excepting the one of Myrtle Collins.

The pictures he had taken were quite good, composed well, with the camera held steady and even. He seemed to prefer symmetry, even to the point of often adopting a perfectly dead-on perspective, which is usually discouraged in photography classes, but which can be used to create an interesting visual effect.

But there was something else that had bothered me about his pictures, and it hit me as I looked around – all of his pictures missed the really spectacular or noteworthy views.

He had taken a couple of snapshots of the pavilion, and I stood at the exact spot where he had, but his photo pretty much included only the table, with a sliver of the woods beyond it. In fact, the camera was pointed completely in the wrong direction in my opinion as an avid amateur

64

photographer.

My heart went cold as the idea hit me and my hand flew to my mouth as my eyes started to tear with the shock – it was as if he was taking a picture of an imaginary person who was looking at the scenery that was to be admired. *Was he seeing dead people,* like in that movie Sixth Sense?

Jack Mulroney

I sat in a diner, thoroughly enjoying a bowl of steaming hot Louisiana chicken gumbo, despite my misgivings, which were really not about the hygiene. As you well know, chili and gumbo typically lead to certain deliberate and wicked devilishness on the chef's part, which does not make itself apparent until long afterwards.

The young Indian cook had jazzed up a can of commercial soup with fried eggplant, potatoes, leeks and cilantro in front of my very eyes, and believe me, it tasted delicious, especially to a weary traveler far away from home on a brisk fall evening. The thick slice of whole wheat bread at the bottom was a very nice, unexpected touch, and spoke of a cook who dared to break tradition.

I was idly flipping through some of the other photos as I ate, without discerning any value in pursuing the trail further. A few were taken off the stern of the ferry that ran between Cape May in New Jersey and Lewes in Delaware.

The one-way fare for a car and its driver was $36 from March through November, and honestly I thought that it would have been out of Jack's price range, but records confirmed that Jack Mulroney had indeed taken the Subaru wagon from Cape May to Lewes, and that he was travelling alone.

I was puzzled by something else that we'd discovered by examining the cell-tower records in the region for his phone. Bearing in mind that there was no way of really knowing that it was he who had the phone, Jack had started out of Sea Bright late in the morning of Tuesday September 30, and had stayed in the general vicinity of Bass River until the evening of Sunday October 5.

Later that night, he'd made his way south down the Garden State Parkway to Cape May, turned around, and headed back north on the Parkway until he was almost halfway back to Bass River, and then turned back south again, finally stopping at a rest area for the night shortly after midnight.

Late the next afternoon, he'd boarded the ferry for an 80-minute ride to Lewes. Around the time he boarded, the phone was shut off, and was not turned back on until he was in Smyrna, Delaware, which was more than halfway up the Delaware coastline. This was very peculiar, since if that was where he wanted to end up, it would have been a heck of a lot cheaper and quicker for him to have simply taken the Atlantic City Expressway west, which would have put him on I-95 South past Wilmington, and then a short hop down Route 13 to Smyrna. Instead, he had driven a huge U down South Jersey and up most of Delaware.

He then spent the night at the Smyrna Rest Area. If that conjures up images of your average truck stop on just about any interstate, let me educate you. You probably have seen families of victims of traffic fatalities build makeshift memorials, at the scene of the accident, to their dear departed. The Delaware Department of Transportation, the Chesapeake Chapter of Mothers Against Drunk Driving and a few other organizations collaborated to build a beautiful park in Smyrna, which includes a pathway outlined with bricks inscribed with the names of traffic fatalities.

It was at that park where Jack spent two nights. Did he lose a loved one in a traffic accident in Delaware? But exploring that possibility would have to wait until the next morning.

The next morning, Jack visited the Bombay Hook National Wildlife Refuge, which was where he'd taken the pictures of the Subaru Legacy wagon on a dirt road that wound its way through parts of the 16,000 acre park, most of which is tidal salt marsh. It is used by migrating birds and is closed from sunset to sunrise, prohibiting any camping or overnight stays.

Interestingly, at the refuge Jack had taken only the picture of the car and one of a picnic table and bench overlooking a lake. The picture he had taken in Bass River was also that of a picnic table and bench, and glancing at the picture taken on the ferry, I saw that right underneath the flag on the stern was a bench. There was also a picture of a bench at the Smyrna rest area.

My cell phone rang – it was Ravi. "Hey, I take it that you didn't get the message I left for you?"

No, I replied. I had been driving through some back roads, and probably missed that call. I would check my voice mail and emails after dinner, I promised him.

"Well, now that I got you on the phone," he said, "you might as well hear the bad news. We got back the DNA results, and that finger does not appear to match any of the stuff that you got off the camera, cell phone or the apartment."

It had taken the FBI laboratory in Quantico longer than usual to retrieve usable DNA from that finger which had been fairly well digested in the bear cub's stomach. I had fully expected them to report that it could not be done, but not getting a match was definitely a let down. "All right then. I'll head on back." If it wasn't Mulroney, then there was obviously no point in continuing this wild-goose chase.

"Hold on," Ravi said as I tried to dejectedly hang up. "I got a name for you."

I had asked him to identify Upton Wallaby's grandson, who had died in the line of duty in Afghanistan, meaning to ask my pastor to mention him during Sunday services, especially since Mr. Wallaby seemed to be a bit out of touch with the world around him.

"Here we go – Jack Mulroney."

"Jack Mulroney is the guy that I had been spooring all this while," I said wearily. "You should know that, of all people, Ravi!"

"Jack Mulroney is the *kid's* name," Ravi said quite evenly.

"*Just what are you saying?*" I shouted in exasperation, much to the consternation of the Indian chef and a smattering of patrons. All that I needed now was for Ravi's normally sharp brain to be in need of a total reboot.

"Jack Mulroney, Jr. is the grandson," said Ravi, thankfully oblivious to my tone. "Upton Wallaby was divorced from his wife Dorothy, nee Mulroney. They had a son, Jack

Wallaby, who after the divorce went by Jack Mulroney, but an official change of name was never filed, and some of his records list him as Wallaby and others as Mulroney"

So that was why we could never get a solid latch on him.

"Anyway, Jack Mulroney, Jr. is that son's only kid," said Ravi, "and he was only 19 when he died in Afghanistan on September 15th – shot by friendly fire."

Epilog

Like I said at the start, I work on suspicious deaths, only some of which I solve, others I fail to do so. I failed to finger the owner of that finger, but it wasn't because I didn't try hard enough. It was not as if I had missed that large flashing red arrow pointing to the culprit, but it because there was no arrow of any sorts in this case.

We collected a lot of information about Jack Mulroney, now that we had his real name and Social Security Number, and could pretty much trace his entire life. He had been raised by his mother, but had reconnected with his father later in his life. He married his high-school sweetheart, who sadly died giving birth to Jack, Jr.

He waited until after his son's graduation from high school to remarry, but that union lasted less than a year, culminating in an uncontested divorce, with no children. During that time, his son had opted to reside with his grandfather, Mr. Upton Wallaby, until he enlisted to fight the war in Afghanistan.

The two Mulroneys, father and son, had made a final bonding trip before the deployment to Afghanistan, camping at various places that had must have held special, fond memories for both.

Jack Jr. had been assigned to support the A10 bomber, which I had observed practicing low-level bombing runs at the Warren Grove Air-to-Ground gunnery range.

Both the Bombay Hook National Wildlife Refuge and the Smyrna rest area were about fifteen miles north of Dover Air Force base, which was home to the largest military airlift operations in the United States.

Dover AFB was also the largest mortuary, processing all of the American Servicemen killed in the line of duty.

That explained Jack Sr.'s wild gyrating loops from Bass River to Cape May - by crossing over into Delaware, he would be barreling towards Dover AFB, from where he had given his son to be airlifted off to the Afghan theater of war on July 10, only to have him returned in a flag-draped coffin on September 19th.

Evidently Jack Sr. had retraced that trip after his son's demise. I cannot imagine how excruciatingly painful and poignant that second trip must have been and to be honest, I don't know how he survived it, because under those circumstances I would have not. If that finger found in that bear cub's stomach had turned out to be his, my heart would paradoxically have been much lighter as I write this chapter; instead, I am having trouble keeping a dry eye.

At this point, your guess is as good as any conjecture of my own; but I am convinced that with his only son a war casualty, the boy's mother long gone, an aging father beyond any facilities of recognition, and a recent failed marriage, Jack Mulroney, Sr. had probably come to the conclusion that his entire life right to that point had been rendered null and void, and had simply decided to end it all at Tohickon.

That is, until God realized that maybe He had placed too big a burden on Jack and sent a young, heartbroken Mark Shepard his way, who had recognized the distress of another desperate soul and had quietly intervened to save his life.

After that, most likely Jack Mulroney, Sr. discarded everything to start over a new life somewhere else. Or maybe I will be called again, to tell of a new final chapter; only time will tell. But I think that the kindness of so many strangers must have provided some salve to Jack's troubled life.

I pray that God will have mercy and not continue to keep testing him any more; to paraphrase Anita Bansfield at the Red Bank Courthouse, there's no reason for a person to have to deal with stress like that.

My pastor did say a prayer for Jack Mulroney, Jr., who was surely at the right hand of the good Lord, another for the safety of Jack Mulroney, Sr., wherever he was, and also one for Mr. Upton Wallaby, who didn't even know that he was living in New Hope, PA.

The End